By Stella Hash

PublishAmerica
Baltimore

First printing

ISBN: 978-1-4626-0533-0
PUBLISHED BY PUBLISHAMERICA, LLLP
www.publishamerica.com
Baltimore

Printed in the United States of America

The stars twinkled as Moses, the mouse made his way across the barren field in search of food for his hungry family.

As he moseyed along he noticed a bucket lying on its side. Moses scampered behind a bush just as Laken, the cat dashed out of the bucket.

Laken did not see the little mouse for his curiosity was focused on a group of camels a short distance away. Moses watched as the cat advanced toward them, but something else caught his attention. The smell of sweet grain was floating heavily on the air. Moses stomach rumbled as he made a quick turn and hurried back to get his family. They would feast tonight.

Moses, his wife Nattie, and sister Miriam left their home and ran toward the camels who were resting. Hurriedly, they climbed into one of the camels packs and crouched in a corner for they heard a familiar scratching noise outside. Suddenly a tiny hole appeared revealing Laken, the cat.

Bazel, the youngest camel was startled by the clawing on his pack. Frantically, he scrambled to his feet, and in the process he stepped on Benora's toe, kicked Fiona's shin, and thumped Baubo on the chin.

The noisy commotion woke everyone. The grumbling camels stood and glared at Bazel. Bazel dropped his head and began to apologize for disturbing their rest. He tried to explain about the cat, but he was rudely interrupted.

"Bazel, you are always disruptive. Now that you have woke the entire camp, get ready to go." boomed the voice of Miacca, the lead camel.

The night sky was full of light and the small caravan of camels, people and mice coursed their direction toward a bright shining star in the eastern sky.

The camels gently swayed as they traveled. Bazel's soft tempo lulled the mouse family to sleep.

Suddenly, a strong wind whistled through the pack where Moses and his family slept. Moses awoke with his eyes stinging. Just then the wind tore at the pack lifting its flap and flooding the little family with a coat of sand. Frightened, Moses gathered Nattie and Miriam close to him and led in a hymn, "The wind and the rain will obey his will. Peace, be still. Peace, be still." Their fears were quieted, finding comfort in the song. Bazel and the other camels could scarcely see their nose in front of their face. Miacca spotted a protected place and hurried toward it followed closely by the rest of the caravan. The camels and wise men hunkered down waiting for the storm to pass.

An hour or so crept by and finally the last of the sand swirled away as quickly as it came leaving the sky clear. The moonlight was beautiful, but the special brightness of the star was enchanting... the star of a little king.

Bazel started to rise when he heard a whisper. Looking toward the sound, he stared bold into beady little eyes and opened his mouth to yell.

Moses stepped forward and boldly spoke, "Shh, I'm Moses, don't be frightened. I'm much smaller than you. My family and I came to your pack for food and were trapped by the cat. You saved us and I just wanted to thank you."

Bazel closed his mouth, then opened it to speak, "Well, I suppose you are welcome, my name is Bazel."

Moses replied, "Nice to make your acquaintance, we will get off here if you want us to. However, we would like to see where the star will take you."

Bazel told Moses, "I'm glad to have you aboard, but let's keep it our little secret. I am always in trouble with Miacca and I don't think he would approve."

Just then Miacca rose barking orders to the other camels. The wise men mounted and the group continued their eastward journey.

The three wise men Melchior, Balthazar, and Gaspar discussed their travel and decided to stop at Jerusalem for information. Upon their arrival, they went to see King Herod inquiring of him, "Where is he that is born king of the Jews? We have seen his star and come to worship him."

King Herod did not know. He called his chief priests and scribes together, and asked them where the child would be born.

They said unto him, "In Bethlehem of Judea, for thus it is written by the prophet."

King Herod came privately to the wise men saying, "Go to Bethlehem and search diligently for the young child; when you find Him, send word to me that I may come and worship Him also."

The wise men departed, however they were warned in a dream not to return to King Herod for it would endanger the little king. The small caravan left Jerusalem following the bright star to Bethlehem.

The road was long and the distance far, so Moses, Nattie and Miriam entertained Bazel with songs. Bazel closed his eyes, swaying to the songs and enjoying the singing. When he opened his eyes, no one was in sight. Panic took hold of Bazel. He ran here, he ran there, but could not see them anywhere. Bazel was lost and he was exhausted.

After resting a bit, he plodded on until he saw a stable in the distance. Wearily, he ran toward it. Bazel stumbled and fell to his knees, and the mouse family tumbled out of his pack.

All of them stared in amazement at the bright star shining down on a newborn babe wrapped in swaddling clothes lying in a manger. A small sweet hand reached out and touched Bazel's cheek warming his heart and soul. He felt at peace and rejoiced with exceeding great joy, for he knew this was the infant king they had been searching for.

The wise men with joy did behold,
Brought Him gifts of frankincense, myrrh and gold.
On bended knees with heads bowed low,
Worshipped the little king whom they loved so.
Even the heavens sang of Jesus birth,
Praise be to God for his presence on earth.

Would you like to see your manuscript become a book?

If you are interested in becoming a PublishAmerica author, please submit your manuscript for possible publication to us at:

acquisitions@publishamerica.com

You may also mail in your manuscript to:

**PublishAmerica
PO Box 151
Frederick, MD 21705**

www.publishamerica.com

CPSIA information can be obtained
at www.ICGtesting.com
Printed in the USA
LVIC04n1542231013
358276LV00008B/85

9 781462 605330